CHICAGO PUBLIC LIBRARY
HAROLD WASHINGTON LIBRARY
BUSINESS/SCIENCE/TECHNOLOGY
400 S. STATE ST. 4TH FLOOR
CHICAGO IL 60605

Fast Facts About Dogs

Fast Facts About FRENCH BULLDOGS

by Marcie Aboff

PEBBLE
a capstone imprint

Pebble Emerge is published by Pebble, an imprint of Capstone.
1710 Roe Crest Drive
North Mankato, Minnesota 56003
www.capstonepub.com

Copyright © 2021 by Capstone. All rights reserved. No part of this publication may be reproduced in whole or in part, or stored in a retrieval system, or transmitted in any form or by any means, electronic, mechanical, photocopying, recording, or otherwise, without written permission of the publisher.

Library of Congress Cataloging-in-Publication Data is available on the Library of Congress website.
ISBN 978-1-9771-2453-1 (library binding)
ISBN 978-1-9771-2496-8 (eBook PDF)

Summary: Calling all French bulldog fans! Ever wondered about a French bulldog's personality? Want to find out the best way to care for this type of dog? Kids will learn all about French bulldogs with fun facts, beautiful photos, and an activity.

Image Credits
Capstone Press/Karon Dubke, 20; Getty Images/adoc-photos/Corbis via Getty Images, 8; iStockphoto/gollykim, 17; Shutterstock: 135pixels, 15, Branislav Nenin, 5, CREATISTA, 10, Eric Isselee, cover, Fotyma, back cover, kavalenkava, 18, Kwiatek7, 16, Mary Swift, 6, tsik, 13, Ugorenkov Aleksandr, cover (right), Unchalee Khun, 11, Vera Petrunina, 12, WilleeCole Photography, 7, yhelfman, 9

Artistic elements: Shutterstock: AKV, Anbel

Editorial Credits
Editor: Megan Peterson; Designer: Sarah Bennett; Media Researcher: Kelly Garvin; Production Specialist: Tori Abraham

All internet sites appearing in back matter were available and accurate when this book was sent to press.

Table of Contents

Friendly Frenchies 4

French Bulldog History 8

Frenchies at Home 10

Keeping French Bulldogs Healthy 14

Caring for French Bulldogs 16

Fun Facts About French Bulldogs 18

    Make a Dish Towel Dog Toy 20

    Glossary 22

    Read More 23

    Internet Sites 23

    Index 24

Words in **bold** are in the glossary.

Friendly Frenchies

French bulldogs want to be your friend! Fans call these loving dogs Frenchies.

Frenchies love to clown around. They like to play games and chase balls. They like to have their bellies rubbed. Sitting on your lap makes them happy. Frenchies make great company.

Frenchies have bat-like ears and large heads. Their faces are flat. Deep folds of skin surround their short noses. Their short fur comes in many colors. White, tan, and **brindle** are common.

French bulldogs look a lot like English bulldogs. But Frenchies are much smaller dogs. They weigh under 28 pounds (12.7 kilograms). They stand between 11 and 13 inches (28 and 33 centimeters) tall.

English bulldog

French bulldog

French Bulldog History

In the 1800s, people in England **bred** a toy-sized bulldog. These little dogs kept people company.

The bulldogs sat on lace makers' laps as they worked. Lace makers moved to France with the dogs.

The French people loved the dogs. They called them French bulldogs. Soon French bulldogs came to the United States. They became very **popular**. Frenchies are still popular today.

Frenchies at Home

Frenchies are happy in big and small families. They love children. They are usually **polite**. They also play well with other animals.

Nothing much bothers a Frenchie. They are easygoing dogs. French bulldog puppies can be frisky. Older Frenchies are **calmer**. All Frenchies are happy sitting close to you.

French bulldogs are great pets for small spaces. They live well in apartments. They also live well in houses. Frenchies do not need a lot of **exercise**. A short walk every day keeps them healthy.

French bulldogs don't bark much. They sometimes bark at strangers. They like to "talk" in their own way. Frenchies snort and gargle. Sometimes they sound like they are singing!

Keeping French Bulldogs Healthy

French bulldogs should visit the **veterinarian** every year. Frenchies can have breathing problems. This is because of their short noses. Hot weather makes it harder for them to breathe.

The vet will check a Frenchie's nose and lungs. The vet will also check the dog's heart, eyes, and ears. French bulldogs live about 10 to 12 years.

Caring for French Bulldogs

French bulldog puppies should be trained early. This helps them stay out of trouble. Sometimes they are slow to train. They don't always like to listen! Reward them with food or toys.

Frenchies can be bathed monthly. Make sure to wash and dry their skin folds. Brush their fur once a week. Trim their nails before they get long. Long nails can be painful.

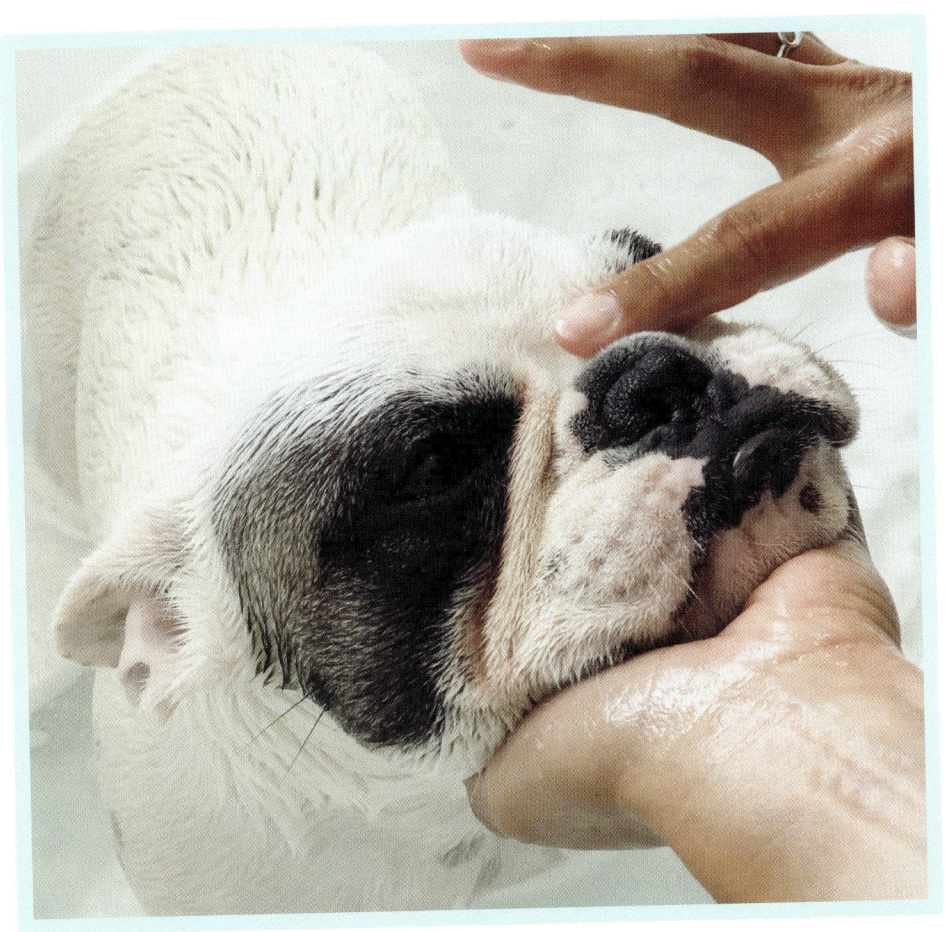

Fun Facts About French Bulldogs

- French bulldogs are the fourth-most popular dog in the United States.

- French bulldogs can't swim. They should not be alone by pools or bodies of water.

- Frenchies do not like to be **scolded**. They get more upset than other dog breeds.

- The first Frenchies had rose-shaped ears.

- Gary Fisher is a famous French bulldog. His owner was the late Carrie Fisher. Gary has 180,000 followers online!

Make a Dish Towel Dog Toy

What You Need:

- scissors
- three dish towels

What You Do:

1. Cut two 1-inch (2.54-cm) wide strips from the short end of one towel.

2. Bunch the three towels together.

3. Take one strip. Tie the strip firmly around one end of the bunch.

4. Braid the towels together.

5. Tie the second strip firmly around the end of the braid. Toss it to your Frenchie!

Glossary

breed (BREED)—to mate and raise a certain kind of animal

brindle (BRIN-duhl)—a coat pattern with specks and streaks of light and dark markings

calm (KALM)—quiet and peaceful

exercise (EK-suhr-syz)—physical activity done in order to stay healthy and fit

polite (puh-LITE)—having good manners

popular (POP-yuh-lur)—liked or enjoyed by many people

scold (SKOLD)—to tell a person or a pet in an angry way that they have done something wrong

veterinarian (vet-ur-uh-NAYR-ee-uhn)—a doctor trained to take care of animals

Read More

Bozzo, Linda. *I Like French Bulldogs!* New York: Enslow Publishing, 2017.

Hansen, Grace. *French Bulldogs*. Minneapolis: Abdo Kids, 2017.

Woodland, Faith. *French Bulldogs*. New York: AV2 by Weigl, 2019.

Internet Sites

American Kennel Club
https://www.akc.org/dog-breeds/french-bulldog/

Animal Planet
http://www.animalplanet.com/breed-selector/dog-breeds/non-sporting/french-bulldog.html

Dogtime
https://dogtime.com/dog-breeds/french-bulldog#/slide/1

Index

body parts, 6, 14, 17

care, 14, 16–17, 19

exercise, 4, 12

feeding, 16
fur, 6, 17

history, 8–9, 19

lap sitting, 4, 8

safety, 19
size, 7, 8

training, 16